The Adventures of Strawberry Shortcake

Random House  New York

and Her Friends

by Alexandra Wallner • Illustrated by Mercedes Llimona

Library of Congress Cataloging in Publication Data: Wallner, Alexandra. The adventures of Strawberry Shortcake and her friends.
SUMMARY: The Strawberry Kids make an unusual scarecrow to frighten birds away from their crops. [1. Scarecrows–Fiction]
I. Title. PZ7.W15938Ad [E] 79-5148 ISBN: 0-394-84319-3 (trade) ISBN: 0-394-94319-8 (lib. bdg.) Manufactured in the United
States of America. 4 5 6 7 8 9 0

It was a beautiful summer day in the berry patch at the edge of the woods. The Strawberryland Kids were looking over their crops, and they were all very happy with what they had grown.

"Hmmmmmmmmmmm," said Strawberry Shortcake, who was standing next to one of her juicy, ripe berries. "These berries are almost as big as I am. I will have to get Huckleberry Pie to help me pick them and get them to my house. I'll make more jams and jellies than I ever did before. There will be lots to sell at the market."

Not far away, Raspberry Tart was sitting beside the
raspberry bush, where she could usually be found. She was
feeling very pleased with herself.

"Just look at those ruby-red berries," she said. "Nobody
but me, queen of the raspberry bush, could raise such
wonderful raspberries. My friends will be very jealous of
the jams *I'm* going to make this year."

Under the blueberry bush, Blueberry Muffin was washing her aprons in the big, chipped white cup with the blue stripe around it. Her aprons always seemed to get stained with berry juice so fast!

"The blueberries really look good this year," Blueberry said to Apple Dumplin'. "I must start making some jelly as soon as I find the recipe. Then we will have such delicious jelly to share with our friends, won't we, Dumplin'?"

Apple Dumplin' was the baby of the group and lived in the hollow of the crab apple tree. She smiled at Blueberry and then curled up to take a nap on the bed of moss that Blueberry had fixed for her under the toadstool.

All the Strawberryland Kids were looking over their
crops. Everyone, that is, except Huckleberry Pie and Plum
Puddin'. They were sitting together at the edge of the
stream that bubbled by the berry patches.

"Did you know," said Plum Puddin', while writing in
his notebook, "that I have found ten ways to make my plum
crop bigger and better? My plums are growing so big and
fat that I will need all of my friends to help me harvest them.
We will have more than we need for the whole winter."

"Hmmmmmm, isn't that interesting?" mumbled Huckleberry Pie. All he cared about was taking naps along the river bank.

"You should try growing huckleberries like I do," he said. "All you have to do is hope for rain. The bushes grow by themselves."

At that very moment, as the Kids were admiring their fruit and making big plans, two Berry Birds had their own big plans for the crops.

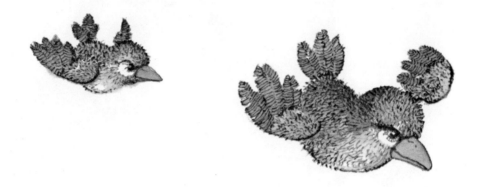

High over the fields and the woods, Buster and Blackie were circling around. They were always looking for the juiciest berry patches.

"I know where to get the best berries around here for miles," bragged Buster. "I've been keeping my eye on them, and the way I figure it, they should be just right for eating today."

"You always were good at knowing the best places to eat," said Blackie. "You gonna keep it a secret?"

"Nah, there's plenty for both of us," said Buster. "Just follow me."

Buster and Blackie flew lower and lower, right down to the edge of the forest where the berry patches were.

"Look at those large strawberries!" said Buster, as he swooped down on the patch and landed on the biggest strawberry plant.

"And look at those raspberries and blueberries!" said Blackie, as he began eating the berries.

"Eeeeeeek!" yelled Strawberry Shortcake, dropping her hoe and running behind a large strawberry.

"My beautiful berries!" yelled Raspberry Tart, who was now hanging on to a branch of her bush. She was really getting tossed and shaken by the birds.

"Get away, you nasty birds!" shouted Blueberry Muffin, grabbing Apple Dumplin' and running behind the cup.

The birds pecked and clawed and stabbed at the berries until they were so full they could hardly lift themselves to fly away.

"Thanks for the grub," shouted Buster as the two birds flew away. "We'll be back for more tomorrow. Ha, ha, ha."

"Is everyone all right?" yelled Plum Puddin' as he and Huckleberry Pie ran to see what had happened.

"Just look at what those nasty Berry Birds did to our crops," said Strawberry Shortcake.

"What a mess!" said Huckleberry Pie.

"Those nasty birds ate half of my raspberries, not to mention what they did to my hair," said Raspberry Tart.

"Dumplin' and I have never been so scared," said Blueberry Muffin. "And the birds said they'd be back tomorrow."

"We'd better hide next time," said Huckleberry Pie. "When they're through with the berries, they might come after us!"

"We should find a safer place," said Blueberry Muffin. Dumplin' was holding on to her apron.

Huckleberry Pie nodded his head and said, "We can't stay here and be safe."

"We'll have to find another place to grow our crops," said Plum Puddin'.

"No we won't," said Strawberry Shortcake, jumping up on a giant mushroom. "If we run away from the Berry Birds, we will always be running away from something. We have all worked hard on our crops, and we have a right to enjoy them. Let's not let those birds bully us. Let's work together and fight them! What do you say?"

The Kids were quiet for a moment and thought about this.

"Strawberry is right,"
said Blueberry Muffin.
"We must find a way
to scare the birds
away. But how?"
They thought and
thought but no one
had any ideas.

Then Strawberry Shortcake snapped her fingers.

"What's the scariest thing we know?" she asked.

"The big black cat who lives in the farmhouse across the field," said Raspberry Tart.

Everyone nodded. They all feared the cat more than anything, even the Berry Birds.

"But how do we get the cat to help us?" asked Blueberry Muffin.

"We don't," said Strawberry Shortcake. "We'll make a pretend cat instead. I have a plan, but everyone has to do exactly as I say."

"Why should we do what *you* say?" said Raspberry Tart.

"Do you want the Berry Birds to come back and steal the rest of your berries and mess up your hair again?" said Strawberry Shortcake.

Raspberry Tart fingered her curls. "Well, no," she said.

Strawberry Shortcake made a quick sketch in Plum Puddin's notebook and then said, "Everyone must find these things:

                  Blueberry—two buttons
                  Huckleberry—a black ribbon
                  Raspberry—some string

"Plum Puddin' and I will try to find some black cloth. When we have found everything, we will meet here. Don't waste any time. We must work fast."

"We'll trust you, Strawberry," said Blueberry Muffin. "You always have good ideas."

"Then let's go," shouted Strawberry Shortcake, as she jumped down from the mushroom and led the Kids across the field in the direction of the farm.

At the edge of the farm, by the old wood fence, the Kids split up.

Down at the far end of the barn, the fence ran around the pigpen. Strawberry Shortcake and Plum Puddin' had spotted a black rag hanging over the fence rail there. They crept up to the pigpen. At the fence, right where the rag was hanging, Old Willy, the biggest, fattest, meanest pig on the farm, was poking around in the dirt.

"We'll have to wait for him to move," whispered Plum Puddin'.

"We can't wait," said Strawberry Shortcake. "We have to act fast."

While Old Willy was grunting and poking and thoroughly enjoying himself, Plum Puddin' and Strawberry Shortcake scurried around the fence post.

Then Strawberry Shortcake climbed onto Plum Puddin's shoulders and tugged at the rag.

"It's stuck!" she whispered.

"Pull harder," said Plum Puddin'.

Just then, Old Willy thought he heard something. He stopped grunting and poking and made the meanest pig face you ever saw. He was looking right at the rag.

By this time Strawberry Shortcake had managed to tug the rag free, and it had fallen right on top of them. They ran away across the field with it over them.

Old Willy watched this strange sight. Then he flopped down in a quiet corner of the pen and decided that he needed a long rest.

At the farmhouse, Blueberry Muffin crept from room to room, looking for the sewing basket that belonged to the farmer's wife. She went through the mousehole tunnels so she wouldn't be seen. Blueberry Muffin knew she could find the two buttons she needed in the sewing basket, but where was it?

She searched the living room and dining room and finally she found it upstairs in the bedroom. She climbed inside the basket. There she found just what she was looking for.

"This red-and-white-striped button is nice," she said. "It reminds me of peppermint candy. And I'll borrow the yellow one here. It looks like a lemon drop."

She threw them out of the basket and then hopped out herself. She carried the buttons on her head and ran for the nearest mousehole.

It was very dark in the mousehole, and Blueberry Muffin had a hard time finding her way. Just as she was rounding a corner, she saw a pair of eyes staring at her out of the darkness.

"Eeeeeeeek!" she cried, dropping the buttons.

"Don't hurt me, don't hurt me," cried a little voice.

"I won't hurt you," said Blueberry Muffin. "Don't you hurt *me*. Who are you anyway?"

"I'm Amelia Mouse," said the timid voice.

"Don't be afraid, Amelia," said Blueberry Muffin, patting Amelia's paw.

"Thank you, you're very kind," said Amelia.

"Can you help me get out of here? I think I'm lost," said Blueberry Muffin.

"Just hop on my back and hold tight," said Amelia.

Blueberry Muffin picked up the buttons and climbed on Amelia. Not only did she get a ride home, but she had made a friend, too.

Huckleberry Pie thought that the most likely place for him to find a scrap of ribbon would be in the large trash barrel the farmer kept by the back porch of the house. He climbed the steps and jumped feet first into the barrel.

"I wish I could have stayed back at the stream," he said to himself.

He rummaged all around the large barrel and finally found a piece of ribbon.

"It's red and green," he mumbled. "But it will just have to do."

He wound the ribbon around his waist, climbed out of the barrel, and headed for home.

The last one to find what she was looking for was Raspberry Tart. She searched in the shed and by the chicken coop and the pig trough.

"Strawberry must think string grows on trees," Raspberry Tart mumbled to herself. "I've looked everywhere but the barn. I might as well look there, too. It's the only place left."

She crept quietly around the corner of the barn until she saw a large space between the boards. Then she slipped inside.

Where do I start looking? she thought.

She looked by the bales of hay in the corner and alongside the horses' stalls. Finally she came to some grain sacks.

She rounded the corner of a big sack slumped against the others and there she found what she was looking for.

"String!" she said and clapped her hands.

She started rolling the string into a ball. She was
working so hard and was trying to loop it so carefully that
she did not look up at all.

Suddenly, as she came around the corner of the sack she
felt very strange.

She looked up and there were two huge, fierce yellow
eyes looking right at her. It was the horrible black cat, and
he was smacking his lips.

"Eeeeeeeek!" shrieked Raspberry Tart as she grabbed the
string and ran behind some grain sacks. Just in time too,
because the cat's big black paw with its sharp claws fell
right where she had been standing only a moment before.

"Whew, that was close," said Raspberry Tart.

She snuck through the grain sacks and found the space
between the boards where she had crawled into the barn.

"Next time, Strawberry can look for her own string,"
said Raspberry Tart as she hurried toward the berry patch.

Raspberry Tart was the last to come back. The others had already gathered by the giant mushroom. Strawberry Shortcake was busy making lists and drawing sketches with Plum Puddin's help. Everyone else eagerly waited to hear what was going to happen next.

"First," said Strawberry Shortcake, pointing to a drawing, "we have to make a skeleton like this. We'll use sticks, and we'll tie them together with all that strong string that Raspberry found. We have to work fast because we have to be finished with everything by tomorrow."

The Kids gathered the sticks they needed and stacked them in the berry cart.

Finally Strawberry Shortcake said, "Okay, that's enough. Let's take them over to the oak tree."

Everyone helped pull and push the cart to the oak tree at the edge of the woods where the berry patches were.

Then they lifted the sticks and tied them into something that looked like a simple skeleton, just like the sketch Strawberry Shortcake had drawn in the notebook.

"This will never work," said Raspberry Tart.

"Of course it will," said Blueberry Muffin. "All you have to have is a little faith. What next, Strawberry?"

"We have to do some sewing on the rag. We will need the posts that hold up your clothesline, Blueberry," said Strawberry Shortcake.

Blueberry's clothesline posts were really large sewing needles that Blueberry and Strawberry had found. The line itself was sewing thread.

The Kids worked so hard that they almost didn't notice it was getting dark.

"Oh dear, what will we do?" said Blueberry Muffin when she began to have trouble seeing. "Soon we will have no light to work by."

"Leave it to me," said Strawberry Shortcake. Then she spoke to the fireflies, who agreed to stand by and give them light.

The Kids worked all night. First they sewed the buttons on the rag to look like eyes. Then they sewed on pieces of string to look like whiskers. Then they tied the ribbon around their pretend-cat's neck. It was all very hard work because they were so small and their cat was so big.

Finally Strawberry Shortcake said, "I think we're finished now." They all stepped back to look at their work. Raspberry Tart, who had fallen asleep, woke up.

"Eeeeeeeek!" she screamed. "It looks just like the black cat at the farm." She was remembering her close call.

"It does looks real," said Blueberry Muffin.

Strawberry Shortcake nodded. "If that doesn't scare those nasty Berry Birds away, nothing will."

Just then she saw Buster and Blackie circling overhead, getting ready to swoop down on the berry patches for their breakfast.

"Hurry," shouted Strawberry Shortcake. She put Apple Dumplin' in the head part because she could screech like a cat. The rest of them got underneath their cat and held up the skeleton made of sticks.

"It's really dark in here," said Raspberry Tart. "I hope we know where we're going."

Whoosh, came the birds, pecking and gobbling up berries.

"Forward," whispered Strawberry Shortcake.

They moved from behind the oak tree to where the birds could see them in full view.

"Screech, Dumplin'," whispered Strawberry.

"Waaaaaaaaaaaaaaaah," screamed Dumplin'.

The trick worked. The birds somersaulted out of the berry bushes in a flurry.

"A cat!" shouted Blackie.

"Let's get outa this place!" yelled Buster.

The Kids peeked out and saw that the birds were really scared of them. They were so happy!

"Let's move forward a little more," said Plum Puddin', and they did.

The birds flew straight up into the sky, squawking all the way.

"I ain't coming back here!" cried Buster.

"Me neither," said Blackie.

The Kids came out from hiding and laughed and laughed.

"I guess we showed those nasty birds who's boss around here," said Strawberry Shortcake.

"Thanks to you and Plum Puddin'," said Blueberry Muffin.

"Now I can get back to the stream," said Huckleberry Pie, dusting himself off.

"And I can fix my curls. They're a mess," said Raspberry Tart as she patted her hair.

"Wait, everybody. Will you help me clean up the berry patches first?" asked Strawberry Shortcake.

They all agreed, and when they were finished, Strawberry Shortcake gave a big party to celebrate.